A Place In Life

Bobby David

Published by Bobby David, 2024.

A PLACE IN LIFE

First edition. May 22, 2024.

ISBN: 979-8224271085

Written by Bobby David.

Table of Contents

With love.

To Joyce Kalake and her team. For fathoming the ghost carriages of our ignoramus pasts to unladen a few schooled minds.

Epilogue

A place in life.
    Tuned to the algorithm of God's intent so are the perfect days of our lives. Like much bellowing do upset the hearth. There is a thing we need more than any form of value in life.

Just a place in life.

A place that can help us do mete and do tell if we made it or missed it. We all need it. There is a thing we need most and we need much direly as sincerely. More dire than love and yet more profound and better than wisdom and understanding and that is still; a place in life.

The key thing being right now; where should you be?

There is a place where your ease and peace of mind are, and until you are one with your placing and timing. It all becomes brutally fatal. You might be the wisest or the strongest at what you do but when not well placed we end in dire ties. Like a choice ship upon the high seas or a massive airplane in the air. We do know when we are well placed and we are at it. For all things gel well and we do not cumber much to occupy.

Since the first day young Thabo could tell.

He did from the beginning, for from his first day at school he brought home a teacher. In all essence in trying to go get an education; he was pursued by education. And from orientation he did bring his mother a graduate. In trying to find out about going to school; he did bring home an education source. He was a whiz at what he was doing. For it was his due time to do go to school and he did go and it all came to pass and this is his story.

The First Day

Sincerely.

In the eighties there was no first day.

There was no first day for school, for the absentia of much parenting did leave a gap yawning for any to do sit and ask. For who would be much cumbered about the much ado about change of uniforms or addition and subtraction of the length of trousers or the design of school jerseys or padded tracksuits. When the results of the pupils leave a lot to be pored in to. T-shirt or golf shirt or bucket hats. They did spent their days away from their kids in the solitude of their not yeaning enterprise; farming.

The rain or God they could not tell. The clouds like a terrible messenger did came mounted with much terror and vehement signs of a due rain yet all fields even of the valiant of men did lay fallow. Yet the more as before they were ever farming. And it meant eyeing the feeble of flocks daily to bodily aid them and coax them on; lest one like a spent song would end up speaking self as a past; a past to say I used to be a farmer. A thing that did open a niche, a niche of unparented children though their bearers did live. At best the luckiest for a neighbor they had a grown pupil, who for the term of the drought would be burdened with responsibility of parenting their siblings and the kin's as the distant neighbor by a long rope. A thing that gave birth to a deliberate pattern where half the class would make it thrice to school any given week owing to the design of the menu. Being a season of draught: there were no negotiations about shared school bills and the parents did care, but were absent none the less; yet the government did try to subsidize all thing s even to being excused by all means from paying any form of school fees.

They did wait and eye the sky.

It presented the situation of unfaithful messengers. For though the clouds were sent with much visible rain they did never let go even a few promising drops. These are the years donkeys did loose their fur and did parade skeletal in their bare skins.

There was no visible reason for it all.

Playing teacher was a dire hope. It was a dire hope that at least half the class would return. So one may continue the clemency of coaxing the aged and gently edging on the young in hope they would by a certain mystery to see their way in to junior school. One did desire they would do desire or at least by default be drafted in. It was not just a dutiful thing to educate; for in the dire morning many had to be given a quick bath outside to quite down the brewing smell of human neglect religiously. A cold bath meant a possible abandoning and an eclectic absence of many others to try to round up the missing lot.

Every term end one hoped they would return.

Return from the ideals of much idleness born of the plenteous adventures of the African scape. Where one could be pulled out of school to be a nurse for her mother to her young brothers and sisters or to be employed. To play the treason of employee often to a well doing uncle to herd or shepherd his flock while his own children are busied at school. An ought only manifesting self repercussive when the aged do compare their ideals. Oh! Africa that you knew!

Yet annually the teacher did come and did waited.

Waited in anticipation that the girls would return missed by the axe of festivities. Where flashy bicycles adorned with much of all the colors of insulation tape and much lights and much double cassette radios were paraded to their being prey. And the drought relief providence of the USAID in 'mmatonosa' and the powdered milk would loose them from the easy come mentality. Age, the fathom of puberty and much juvenile intents did mar their chance for most made it to school in the paradox of childhood and maturity. A stage where one's mind is soon blighted by the new rage of hormones.

There is a thing more scary than any form of introduction one would ever have in life. It is the ideal of first assuming school alone the very first day when the whole lot have done come back. Though in the eighties most did not return from the lands which is African English for farms in regular English until the second week.

Yet the avid first comers did eclectically break the first week as the heroes of the registers. A thing that made the very first week of every term a real peachy. Peachy for it was for cleaning and much garbage picking and much games playing as the teachers did add up the ideal numbers to start teaching again. The concerted absentia afforded the first comers an ideal of plashing the first few days in much play until like a good song it gets spent.

Then began the week of giants.

Giants like Potekane, Kedibone, Mosenki and Malombo did not show until then. They did not show for they had to bring a mother or a near kin to reregister them to attempt standard four the seventh or more times for the converted ideals of it being a sports term. A thing that sold the school system cheap for all would like to get most of the cheers and accolades accorded their school. A thing that would heat up the assembly for the most part of the first term as victories earning the individuals enamel coated plates and bowls meant a successful sports term; another synonym for track and field events. It being the first and most active was usually followed by the ball sports season. Simply put, the netball and football season for there was no other sports but the two. Then the third that was the most hated of terms where the most of giants are no where to be found. First for it was singing season and second it was the term for exams. There did go much of the giants to a sabbatical until the preceding term being the first again. And again it would be their first day at school again.

This is the term that if it was not for their school shorts and prevalent hatred for shoes, you would have confused a lot of them for teachers. For many like Papolo and Super and Tipa and Fakane and Manko had to often find a stone to whet the edge of the blunt the make shift scissors to appear assumptive candidates of the pupils mass. They did had often to be coaxed out of the toilet to do even the simplest and earliest of tasks like to attend assembly.

The lot did not just fall on the male culprits but even of a few astounding returnees were a few common faces like Cruise Mjapane, Somhlolo and a few more candid others. These were no longer remembered by their true names but their sporting adorations as one has already discover the names cannot be true.

They did miss the often axe of teenage pregnancy and did labor on for a hope to escape the ideal of a fatally failing school.

What was, was happening to all. For it was not just Maranyane Primary School that was at it but twelve others to be precise in Kanye that had the candid ideal to not just attempt to educate but even try to cause any to discern the value of learning. There was a system that was already serving the people well. After doing standard four a few times and a few other times. It was time to be in the line at TEBA for the South African mines. There the stone ever hardly missed. For it took not a sound mind or an ability to read or interpret: but an able bodied being and that was it.

So, the school as usual did begin. As usual the second week as they did busy the make shift scissors and spasmodically going in to the toilet to do take a smoke or two before the first lesson. A thing that obviously needed the handy mint sweet or the Wilson triple x if one had a little change to spare. So did the giants as the tiny tots do labor to ascertain the ideals of a working school.

There is a welcome.

A kind of welcome that outstays all the welcomes one would ever receive in life.

Speaking for the generation that had never seen the inside of a crèche and let alone kindergarten. There is a welcome they all remember.

It is the welcome of the first day at school. And the first day to the elucidation of all is obviously not the first day you go to school. But one of the first few days at the beginning of the first term. It could not be the real first day. For the first few days did the teachers spend casting lots for the spasmodic additions to make a full class. One needed to start a little over their tally to leave room for much exodus that shall pursue the heat of learning. That is the profound and impaling moment you have to meet the cheer or the lack there of it from your first teacher, for being introduced to the learning of letters is like picking the prick of a yoke. This is the most important of days to many people's lives. For the thing they have become have spewed out of the way school has received them the very first day; that is with the former explanation in mind.

Did it or did it not become their place in life?

Little Thabo so went without the aid of his older brother for he had graduated to junior school the former year. A half bag of surprise rice knit with intricacy to accommodate the handle a half way lower to avoid tripping on it. A piece of wood, a generous metal dish well set in his rendered diminutive repurposed rice bag to cede his stature and he was so as others except for the a bone. He did not carry a wood stick and bone for their induction to fending was not yet set, Thabo for his first day just did bring a dish and his ever handy repurposed bag. He there followed the lot much cumbered by the generously large bag irregularly kicking at his rather roomy dish as it did do much hopping in his slippery carry bag.

Tuesdays were days when the school received bones to aid relief the country of the drought by granting a mass of bones, for a reasonable price to the school of course. And Wednesday was when a few cans were gathered weekly to aid the aluminum rash that spooked the eighties. And this things were just normal like going as a herd to go hunting for cement and bread paper to cover books. It was even the more normal to go can hunting, that is when the parents did not really have a say regarding the terms of running the school or their children's rights.

School was at times cranking.

The first day was when the not so many new pupils came in, in myriad vestures for mostly the lot of them started off without yet having a uniform. It was still a common site, to see even the standard sevens well ironed in long trousers without shoes. As now and then for a dare the headmistress would pull one of them; one of the biggest to refute a thing. With them mostly much munching a lot in to puberty and beyond. They now and then took her on for a dare. A thing that always ended with the engagement of one profound teacher; S'tlhophane, the taunt of being an only young male faring the dare to educate Africa.

Apart from cutting sleeves or legs of trousers. Impressing was yet another weakness that made the daring land too often in hot waters. Instead of a problem she would rather make a presentation of it. For most went to school leaving all parents and elders out at the farms commonly in our English known as lands. Meaning all ought and care was owed to the headmistress and her squadron of teachers. Among the many stunts one could pull, due to lack of parental care was this; being the eighties, it was a fashionable thing to iron on the print of the sugar plastic back on the backs of the school shirts. Or drawing the African chess board or 'mhele' on the back of the shirt with a hot iron.

Both the above said were an offence to suffer a few quick slaps wherever there is an opening before she drags you about with you ear. A thing that needed a bit of patience for she will be pulling one with the prick of her nails. As the bigger lot suffered her quick selective criteria and there and then it was water under the bridge. So would the little new ones now and then be prey to her taunt. For now and then she would take one tiny culprit dressed in an array of colors and announce her disgust for the lack of uniform in front of the whole assembly.

There was a criteria that made one simply qualify owed to the ideal of her being petite. Being of a tiny build and being among the first few in line made you prey. A thing that caused much shuffling and scuffling a lot more than it is necessary in the lines of the assembly. She was just an exemplary leader and that is what set her lovingly in all hearts. And for the headmistress to make it radical, she was supposed to be holding one mid-air to explain that it is not how you dress for school. Of the many forms of clothing she yet the more hated the dungaree the most. For wearing dungaree made one the first pick of the two or three that will suffer the first term welcome.

Thus it cumbered her the first term. But by the second term she would be occupied by marking a chosen few's compositions and letters. A thing that afforded one the more classical embarrassment of having headmistress as the one marking your work. A thing mostly suffered by those doing standard six and seven. For she would come and make a distinction of a few deliberate things like annunciation of 'the' from 'de'. It brought an adventures adrenaline, a spectacle and a chance to break a few careless laughs of the stock that is usually advantaged by being bright at one or all things.

The lot of the mothers and others had to queue for a chance to serve in ipelegeng for two or so months that they can afford a uniform. And switch off from the make shift incentive so that another may afford the former for their child. Often burdened with three or four in primary stage, meaning a whole year and eight months would be needed to sate the demand. So they got in to any form of clothing that can afford them to see through the first year or term in their own terms.

Being well placed, Thabo had the opportune moment that when his brother rose to the junior school rankshe was ripe for primary. So, it afforded his to take his shift of his much tattered uniform. A thing that left him a primary school heritage so thoroughly spent it made him an instant acquaintance. Though being the first day. There in the bustle of much play a solid number of the actual acquaints had already marred or popped a button due to the rigorous nature of African play grounds.

They are full of throwing things.

The kids kept casting things at each other like throwing words or a ball or kicking one another. Games like 'tshetshe' can only be palatable in African play grounds. Games like 'gwaragwara', donkey, skipping wool and skonti ball cannot be mobilized without breaking a sweat. A thing that often brings a stink the teacher would constantly complain about. And even in the dead of winter so cause all the windows to be fully open to the torment of the incumbents of the games and the rest just playing prey. A thing so common yet could not cause the energetic to quit their games much in turn causing the repercussions of winter to cause more damage that it could have ever attempted on its own.

Before even the first assembly they would be out casting ball and already drenching self the much in all delict to school governance. Announcing their arrival with a dire need to whipna lash. Forcing the headmistress to appear for the very first time to many's welcome already with a stick in hand. And the adventurers already with their own teams skipping wool. A deliberate offence they will suffer much the taunt of the teacher for. For the sooner the doors are closed there would rise a hearth. A hearth loosed of their invigorated blood flow. And to them it did not matter much, for the first day is usually for picking litter and sorting a desk and a chair as so goes the whole first week or two.

Mostly a new year brought the surprise of a new teacher but to the new comer who is undiscerning it is all 'greek'. They do come unschooled or without a shared history of their teacher making them vulnerable to any and to all. And it is this day, that finally bedims or enlighten further the excitement of the priced Christmas surprise; a school uniform. A sure set one would endure during the seven first years of their education, that is to say if they can afford the ideal. It all added to the first.

Those that it did not go well for, meant for good they never had a good primary days . And to the lot that it went well, they did acquire tall tales and heroes to go tell home stories about. The unfortunate put to a disposition where they have to elude the teachers for a life time. Yet to those who got a cheerful first day, find closure and purposed desire to be the best at whatever the first day spewed them to be.

School become their place in life.

Heroes they emulate as they cumber the miseducation of play school voluntarily daily playing the teacher with the scantest of abilities. Yet they know who they aspire and are endured with the ideal of they having a perfect well set life. Being in Botswana in the eighties, you either became a primary school teacher or a miner or the illusive ideal a policeman or soldier. With many holding the scant elite of a nursing aid and there and then a nurse. And that was how high ambition could rise you, for all else were in the hands of foreign nationals. From junior school and above.

Cliché.

The primary school teacher was an ideal. An ambitioned position that the blooming were set to fruit. These are they that are play school heroes. They that are often plagued by the conditions of their service and are marred with the aftermath of a failed school system. Unprepared children and a lack of implements to ply their trade with the desired deliverance. They often paint prosperous vistas upon young girls minds to confidently constantly borrow their names every time they had to play teachers in play school. Only if they knew how much of their names is borrowed daily to make a cheer before the fake chalk boards leaned against hideous walls or peradventure a well shadowed tree.

The often escapades of tobacco smoke did mar the toilets the much tainting the air with a strong smell of unprocessed tobacco or 'mabolara' as simply known though of many brands. To understand Africa is to understand simplicity, for toothpaste is simply called Colgate despite their myriad brands and names. Powdered soap is called surf despite the myriad and many brands and forms. And so goes with all things, which ever thing came first is and shall always be. With any horse and trailer donning the name O'Shekotch, a Russian brand heavy duty vehicles here obviously misspelled.

The first day for Thabo was rather welcoming. Received in a class with a full-time teacher and even a TTC intern meant a heaven of astounding possibilities. For it meant they had one aspiring to be a graduate teacher toying with the vistas of her place in life. A thing that meant they would reach far and even play the most daring of first term games. Yet he was at peace as one that has done found his place. A thing that meant he had a lot to aspire and to tell home about.

The Bus Rank

Cankered by the supposed ideal to be a village of the opposition party, mostly owed to being servants to a politician chief. There is a saying in Africa, a saying that was resonate of her. The Setswana saying that says, "Yare kgosi go tlhotsa malata a gogobe." And this saying simply translates; in the instance that the chief limps, the servants crawl. There left much way behind time upon a rock basin once was arrayed the village of Kanye.

There was a thing astounding in the rather development scant village of the Bangwaketse tribe. From upon a rock platter, the spewing of growth has caused the once lofty village to be mainly nestled between hills. Nested between rocks the hilly village of Kanye is not just the headquarters, but the rife center of the Ngwaketse people set aside by their eloquent Tswana annunciation: tje. Desolate of all modernity, she so sat upon a hill for the most part of the beginning of the democratic rule. A stern example of the price of a well held ideal: pride.

The pride of presupposition, has thus dampened this educated village in to the lagging ideal of the most less populous of the country's villages. Though of Africa, Botswana is among the few that were never colonized. She yet has to have her own government hospital or tarred road. And though much abandoned by the wheel of enterprise. This humongous village of it populous ideals have thus spilled from the top of the hill and have in the process of time been favored by the once bypassing trans-kgalagadi highway.

Though with the ramification of reaping the village asunder, much traffic and myriad villages here by the trans-kgalagadi for moment lay aside their luggage to switch their mode of transport or to just transfer to another bus or minibus. Still held on the ideal of the trans-kgalagadi highway. Here is where you can have perfect idea of how roads were constructed back in the days.

There was the generally populous excuse for a bus rank before the decimally primitive mahube store. And there squeezed between it and Gaamangwe General Dealer was the sham called the market by the masses. A tiny metaphor of the name composed of open spaces sparingly roofed to hold a bucket or two of fat cakes and boiled maize combs. And to add salt to the idealism of isolation, a security fence utterly separated the place from the bus rank. A thing that only afforded them the usual roads department customers, for the masses were robbed of those at verge of the bus rank between the market and the bus rank.

There the scantily dressed urchins used to harbor behind sniffing glue and to await the unsuspecting person with any form of visible change to nab or ask by force. Kanye of all the villages is also rife of one thing. People who have gone loco, there are more mad men here than in all villages in the nation combined. And so the scantily dressed young men used to scream with a bag of orange hang over a shoulder.

"Ma-orie!, ma-orie!, ke mang yoo batlang ke motseisa. A n-gafa lesome."

Which directly translates.

"Oranges!, oranges!, who wants to me to help them with their luggage for a price of one pula."

So, they offered their couriering services for one pula as they still pressed on for an opportune one pula to any who needed help to carry their goods to the dilapidated taxies. They themselves charged well over the taxi as it at first charged only sixty thebe. A thing that compensated the anguish one would suffer the much for the paid ride to anywhere near home.

Yet the couriering service was to another exclusive place. The Jwaneng taxi rank. The orange sellers so made an eclectic trip continuously between the about seven stone throws between the two ranks. Though cumbered by much travel. One would say they were robbed the dues of seating by the skimpiness of their dress code. A short pair of trousers and that was about it, for they had earned their way through the rushed masses of bottles and everything to beyond eyeing but just discerning.

Attempting to sell an orange to the odd ball and still attempting the lucrative ferrying offer. That often much quantified their burdens as upon the shoulder slang oranges bag they had to carry a bag or two they offered to help with. And if the supposition of abating self wounding or in avoiding the crashing of one's valuables, one upon the one pula they pay they often have to aid the ferry one way or the other to avoid accidence.

That is upon paying; one has to carry their own luggage in part.

A thing most often suffered by new mothers. For upon the new bundle of joy they would have to come from the SDA hospital with a few amenities that set to accord the ceremonious rituals of receiving a new born. And the bus rank was the connecting point to home village or a distant ward within the village.

The masses of the street sellers and the audio dubbing cassette jockeys preferred to be closer to the buses. Where they would be able to lure much in to an impulsive sale before they compose a formula to work out the mathematics of their budget. So they were snatched in to a quick sale, as the Chinese guy also worked his best Setswana approach. A thing they needed not much for it was still hard to get a cheap watch or "tshasa" the rubbing stuff that was endeared by many. All they need was a brief case, as their much desired stock of "tshasa" ointment was just a few centimeters thicker than a one pula coin. And they made a kill, for many would attempt all rituals before they could reach the hospital door. Owing to the English speaking doctors and the availability of much alternative medicine.

So, the trans-kgaladi, was not even distant but gave a peck not much of a touch but it was almost part of the rank though it did so on its south side. And there on the other side of the rank was the Pitse-E-Ole-Ka-Disale Fruit And Vegetable Tuck-Shop. Much contending with One-More-Time, of the latter function and design.

Though composed of iron sheets, One-More-Time, was the robust of the two. In branding and painting. The former was just pure shiny corrugated iron and of one or the other one could quickly get a bag of oranges to attempt a walking shop. A thing that on its own desired one sure to contend with the surely brutal sun of southern Botswana. So the choosy did go and get their services there at the source but for an orange or two one would avert one of the walking shops from their course of much screaming for a quick sale.

For since nineteen seventy nine, the ideal of the SADC countries basic transportation channel has been held to this day. Here the tarred road bares testament of the laborious burdens she had borne for the wheel of enterprise. Though once a second president was born and raised here, he as the lot of the village could not gel to the end of his rule. Which bares testimony of the much ruins and ghost shops left to the ruin of time.

There began a beautiful thing.

Due to it being the epicenter of a district. All roads of all the little villages about her and the towns have to go through her to reach each other. This Importunity is not even spared the robust mining town of Jwaneng. For the masses to reach this town of hope, they had to make a torrent reeling through the formerly lonesome village of Kanye. Here being a passage borne of her a supposition and a new ideal. That the myriads of strangers passing through, for a coin or two would purchase a morsel. A morsel to sustain them for the remainder of the journey, whether headed home or to the lustrous town of Jwaneng.

Here her nestling upon the junction for a moment made her robust with this enterprising traffic. Coming in or coming out of Jwaneng pouring in to Kanye. And Jwaneng being the key mining town of the Botswana the beloved country.

There was a bus rank.

That is if one would be careless enough to ignore that it was not even paved. If it only had boundaries it would have feign been confused for a play ground, but even the met of it's supposed parameters had no visible tallying. But none the less, to share the ideal of the oracle one would say a gathering ground for the number of minibuses headed to this mining town. Still rank fitted the name for the deliberate gathering there of, was specifically if the minibuses headed only to the mining town of Jwaneng.

Kanye being the amalgamated center from which you can get a direct and intact bus to the said town. Did influence the neighboring villages and towns alike. For one to get to Jwaneng even in the way yonder Kanye was sure of a ferrying minibus from Kanye that could make it to Jwaneng in one piece. For you to reach Jwaneng from any other place through Kanye here you had to swap buses to reach Jwaneng. And it meant a further two hours in the bustle of the much cumbered minibus, of the zeal of the Marchant and the jiggered wares of an intended squatter you had to dodge pricy or hazardous implements all the way. So to conclude this anticipated journey one had for a moment have to relieve his legs of the lag of the former.

Those who had a chicken to catch for a moment they could look in to their carry box but the lot had to scatter to seek a relative or to enter a stall for a priced meal. There was nothing but that to do for there was practically nothing to see. Lecha was a bar that if one would desire to be the taunt of the journey and be at the mercy of the rather violent bus conductors one would dare enter. Not a thing owed to their due cause but the often need of friction to make one pay the right amount to be written a fare ticket. Anticipating an abandoning along the way if the stink one carries or the often violent bloats hashing an involuntary burp did prevail, it could prove be a rather self wounding cause. For if the minibus has abandoned you, the fire of the news would reach both ends of the ranks before you can set a foot upon a cabin.

That is considering then a new car was an unheard of thing, except you get one if the lifts from the South African based miners who also if the groan and taunt of their third or fourth hand shams for vehicles. They were often burdened with a tank or huge plastic for the often enterprise of brewing local concoctions for the merriment if much celebrations or the deliberate other; selling for profit.

They had a dedicated space a Ross road in the other side of the trans-kgalagadi highway. Right opposite Green-pastures General Dealer, a place renown for its fat cakes and vegetable soup. The sophisticated lot sought a chair within the then super modern restaurant side of the s8d general dealer. But the general toms turned aside to a card boxes stall for the indecent stew of tripe or chicken feet to make haste the munching of the brown bread fat cakes. For a place where the stink of the shoe of the robust armpits would not be amplified to the warmth of the microwave warmed soup and the sterling fat cakes from the brooder.

The perfume in deodorant or the roll-on was not yet a common thing. This are the times the apocryphal hand not set a red pin on the Botswana map. The thing with stink is you become aware of it only if someone from outside affords to tell you if it And patch works upon one's father's old clothes afforded the young men to be cumbered in a fashion ideal of the said time; the big size. There Thabo's mother's fame was a rife thing for here renown of her chicken skins soup. Ho8hnow and then she had to fall for chicken livers or necks, the lesser sort of the dejected of the sumptuously feeding was thus the source of her abiding grace.

Though indirectly asked of her recipe an uncandid number of times, she had no staunch answer to ascertain her rivals. For it was obvious that by the time her tripe and fat cakes are done, the other seven or so other boxes stall had the ability to start contending for the customers she could not serve. She had a thing with people one could not distinguish. But she drew the lot of the masses with her abiding kindness and a temperate reach if arm that made all feel graced to be shadowed in her excuse for a shadowed stall. Here indeed the blanket was too short to cover the legs and the head and too narrow for one crouch.

Yet the more life went on.

They just stood there and gobbled the rumen and intestines tripe with a bit of a skin now and then courtesy of the deliberately light chicken skin soup. It was the qualm of the current affairs that drew the masses in rather quickly. For bus drivers are massive reporters for those not taking if speculating a pay. For a free copy of the Daily News, and a jarful of grapevine, so they hurriedly partook of her delicacies as they stood. And when done she would be headed home to the further pick of the axe and a quick purchase of the needed ingredients of tomorrow's sales.

At the crow of the third watch she would be rising early to engage in the gruesome enterprise. Though an uncompromisingly eclectic routine, it afforded her house the escape of the rumble of belly. And the often clinic travels caused by a USAID yellow maize and soya mealie-meal simply dubbed mmatonosa. To the eloquent release of spontaneous release of air that cumbered those who religiously partook of it.

The profound horse feed had made it in to Africa as food aid due to the much plaguing of the draught. These are the years donkeys would labor to walk let alone a weight or load to carry for it would not just collapse but be buried by the weight. The feed was one sure tasty mealy meal but for the high price of embarrassment. For it had a tendency to let go of incontrollable burst of emissions of air. And regulating it meant abandoning the solace of pride, for it would mean now and then you would burst of the butt would crack if you understand what it means. The tearing eloquence of release of the air meant you were at its mercy for the most part for one would not afford to be excused for the needed amount of times. So in 1987, it was almost the schools staple food, with penene, or lentils being the once or twice a week delicacy. Though the sound of the mortar was heard as soughum pounding was so often carried by those hired for the said enterprise. It was rather spasmodic due to the lack of the staple food. The cooks made sure it eluded the masses when it shall be served for it cause much of the loafers to more than necessarily show up.

The thing about lentils, is they tricky even the most wonderful of cooks. For when they can over cook even for a moment they become thick crude. And yet they pack a compaction that often upset the belly in a really windy way. For you could hear literally the wind try to make a pass or whatever it is that is done by metabolism that causes to make one suddenly turn air and bloated and an obvious riot of the belly.

These two. On their own made school days memorable. For one or the other had a few stories of their own regarding mojenje as Bakgatla called the yellow mealies feed for food or they otherwise dubbed it mokhongolo. Even for the penene they had another name being "nkhwisi" of all these, the most awesome of the school delicacies was our staple food soughum porridge mixed with powdered milk, and the obvious lack of compassion or skill to prepare this meal was what made it the beloved of school meals. For you could not finish a dishful without accidentally running on lumps of the powdered milk big enough to make a chewy snack. And the often cause was to excuse them, though I essence harboring them for the lump were the sought after chewy snack of the masses. Everyone was desirous of "lekope" as it was fondly known. Though now and then one would stumble upon one that is entirely made of sorghum compounding to a ruinous disappointment.

1987

Nineteen eighty-seven was a very good year.

Though it had a chilly winter. The kind of winter that cruelly ruptured the heel a few centimeters yonder skin of bare heels and slitting blood spewing harrows causing one to tiptoe the most of a week. Africans!, Hoe come we did not know it needed a simple remedy; shoes. Cast marred and scuttled, though many had not the luxury; the few who did left them at home eyeing mobility during the much self imposed extra-curricular activities. Like a kraal full of young calves, school was a buzz; a buzz of quick thought games at every opportune moment and given chance. The freedom soon earned of the lot that had been herding lambs and calves came with this impediment owed to the blank spaces yet to be field with much bantu education; ignoramus.

Sorry to have began with the most painful of the two usual things that was synonym of new comers of the primary schools. Being naïve of the things of civility, they often cattle post over stayed started standard one ripe for exiting primary school, excusing the English; they just overstayed their herding days to be so late for primary. Yet the much screaming of the headmistress at the top of her lungs abruptly caused many to remember the urgency of education as they entered the school ground. A thing mentioned for the sake of formality. For the school fences then we're like abandoned kraals with much portions of the fence missing in varied places though it was punishable offence to walk through those gaps.

There was a trade.

The troubling trade was wire cars. For the loss was not just suffered by the schools but also Botswana Power Cooperation as Botswana Telecommunications cooperation. Though the wires had to go through the same ritual, the actual car wire frame had to go through the fire to deal the local government paint, the binding wires to deal with plastic cover that deemed to belong to the said cooperation's. Yet even the grave yards suffered this common looting as did the generals masses. They simply had a common enemy; inventive kids.

The much cumbering of this said trade had to be opportune in the harbored of places. Of a conglomerate holding their conniving and engineering of the said products somewhere on a dusty corner barefoot. The much wallowing in the dust to produce the said product soon brought astounding repercussions. For one had to escape unseen and return unseen fundamentally denying the parenting the simple ideal to regulate bathing times. A thing or two in the end did happen. But the first as last was the lasting ideals of a lacking of bathing while continuously wallowing in dust.

Returning to the more severe of the two, simply locally dubbed manga, it was the more painful of two of a kind. The first was a simple trademark of the dry makgadikgadi simply known as makwapa. Symptomized by parched heels resembling the ground of the dried makgadikgadi. That is by myriads of just about heel skin deep checked heels.

Though of heels. It had a tendency of along with heels skin deep Cruses, also upon the foot top to give the resemblance of the former pattern. But manga was when the case suddenly becomes severe. And severity means; when one is walking the simply all of sudden feel a sharp prinking pain that do not identifies self as the issue of a cracked heel a few layers beyond the heel skin. But usually a quick gush of blood help one get that free diagnosis; that they have burst a crack of their heel.

It meant a quick turn around and an absentia of a few days why the first signs abate. Or the continuous streams of the blood can rapture a vein and become a quick cause of hospitalization due to a raptured vein or the other, that is know by the medical inclined. Here school shoes are still rare. For though they cost about s bucks at the Groonavalt store. The little of the pupils though scant, for most of the by the time they do standard four they would have already made blunt a few pair of scissors with stubbles of their own chins. These were mostly the lot that came to school on Monday, Wednesday and Fridays being the days allotted for the sumptuous of the school diet; penene. It still fired formality for the most part they mostly wore long school trousers without shoes. And the beloved of those who came to school much too late were the staunch and short.

These were responsible for ruining the dreams of the athletic and young. For a piece of would was suspended for the masses to pass under to aggregate segments to compete. They did not care of age but the tall ran with the tall and the short with the short regardless. A thing that made the very first term of school a populous one. Unforgiving to the young hopefuls, for apart from it being a sporting term, by the time the second and most painful and cold began. Most of the sporting fraternity would be way back in the forest herding calves waiting for the next year to come and run and play ball yet again.

Despite the vehement exodus still the more the headmistress kept at being steadfast. Even the more encouraging the feeble few. Still screaming at the top of her voice.

"Come along!, come along! Come on, come along."

She was the kind of a leader who was encouraging. Simply known as Come Along, that is under every grapevine of the still schooling and the former incumbents. For though trusted with this undying enterprise, a few that is two or three made it well in to Junior school. For the lot, standard seven was a gateway in to the wheel of enterprise. For much of the abiding school teachers were a dying breed, for they mostly did not make it beyond the primary gates. But there was an army, a breed which had superseded junior and we're college schooled that were coming. Though often suffering the surmise of the old pupils, they yet carried in all excellence bringing forth awesome results.

They were thus tasked instead of the old to take care of the budding shots. To

Much as the smart phones are common among school kids. Then was a hot stone wrapped in cement paper a common ideal. A thing that could in all fondness be shared of a few friends and even compassionate siblings, for a piece of meat or bread in the latter hours of the day back home. For the fire rather than the television was the family epicenter. Meaning the day was spent soliciting for new idioms or telltales that can dampen all current affairs in lore worthy of a good night's sleep. So for a thing to say around the fire at night as the food and water and everything was readied by the one sure wooden fire one thing was rife in the mind. Carrying a fire wood head load down the steep slopes of the hilly village home. While being consumed by the pace of the much laded mother's ready to let go of the burden before ferrying the water bucket along with the lesser for the younger to occupy their scanty baths in the following morning. Though eclectic, it afforded one the needed exercise daily to shout horrid scares to the children of sickness.

When thorns were not yet infected. It was a common thing to see one delicately tearing at his younger sibling or their own foot with a sure thorn to scoop out a prinking stray somewhere in the depths of their foot flesh. And in the latter hours of the self same day they would try it at a game of skonti-ball or gwara-gwara. That is just before the wild was sprayed by makgowa. It was normal to be cruel to dintlhwa and mantsoro after a good rain. For it quickly flame grilled abdomen made for an oily snack. And the locust now commonly known as grasshopper was a conducive meal.

Still this one can say again. 1987 was a very good year.

When it was not unhealthy to pick from another's mouth. Which was often suffered by the little ones who had five thebe to get the bite sized fat cakes. Of a quick nab, one would press hard the incumbent's mouthful to disposes them of this sparingly prepared delicacies.

1987 was indeed good year. It was when the young men walked about with cassette radios. And where one had a double cassette it was a worthy thing to parade about with, for it surely brought about a candid company. Owing to this pass time now and then one uncle or an owed rival would hang by the school gate and end up causing for a quick untimely school assembly to indate the authorities, in this case the male teachers who were a deliberate extension of the headmistress' authority. A job shunned for it meant often contention with the biggest of pupils. The kind that have suffered much self wounding of multiple attempts to trim their beard without the aid of a mirror. Mostly to the lack of a soothing source to weaken the rigor of their stubble; shaving cream.

A PLACE IN LIFE

There was a new pattern due to Kaelo now doing his junior school years. He had to be late daily from the ritual of being the family cook. A thing one would candidly say he had prepared his young brother thoroughly for. For the last two terms of standard seven he was either coming way too late or he would be sunk in his book trying to make the best of the soon vanquished sunlight. A thing that meant he had to read by the ever soot spreading paraffin can lamp; moitaletsi.

Moitaletsi is the home made version of the kerosene lamp. A stingy can and a cord of two pieces of cotton cloth then you are done. All you needed else was to punch a hole any where on the lead any how and pull the cord through the hole in the lead. With about a handful of kerosene a whole week of a blinking wick one would suffer to read due to its often shifting flame that cast too long and often scary shadows. It has a way of amplifying anything but light. Yet if you dare extend the cord a little more than it is necessary it would soon fill the house with hanging soot in a representation of a terrible smoke.

This is one obscene method of lighting. For before you do anything in the morning one had to use their forefinger to dub soot out of their nostrils. A thing that do announce the obvious prevalence of tuberculosis during the eighties; that is apart from the obvious scourge that was then. So, reading a bit early was much better than trying to spot letters in the ever shifting light much owing to the usual space between the mud hut wall and the roof. It did make any given day breezy, for the thin air did make the little flame too much of a vagabond to pursue anything steadfastly for a certain moment in time.

Yet despite the said advantages, the same exam was written by all. Those who read under stars, the street light or the shifty little flames; it all added up to the next entry with or without a silver spoon. So, Kaelo knew for he knew his place in life. That we are not born as who we are meant to be: but we become what we do endeavor to be. Meaning, upon the definition of our purpose; there is also the call to rise and act out our intent and that is what makes all the difference.

It meant Thabo had to be in the office of the cook's help. That is to initiate him to the hazards of the open wooden fire without the startle of burning whole meals. He thus had to occupy the office of the bellows. Though to his disadvantage, he would be pumping mostly using his mouth most of the time. For the job soon eats of the vigor of the shoulders and one tends to find blowing the fire with the mouth a rather relieving act. A job that often means having a charred face, clothes and too often the fingers now and then did endure the sting of a love coal too many. For one has to constantly pry the fire brands to make use of their concerted effort. It is an office that did not just exclusively introduce one to taking minor burns, but also the drench of stepping on live coals taught one a quick lesson of the duty of care. That is if you stepped on a bigger live coal or held a larger live brand's burning part.

The often accidence was a thing one was not supposed to be seated off. That is if they were soon to graduate in to being the family stern cook. For it takes endurance to keep a fire and give a meaningful meal. Among these were things like one's first plastic induced burns. Though an obvious quick fuel that do obviously avail quick results, running plastic is one of the reasons many young often adequate the clinic halls. It just is the way to teach one that hastiness is the often cause of accidence rather than good results. Though one usually learns by their own minor burns, for it has to be cumbered much to burn in the right place due to its running behavior once fully aflame.

This induction in to being the fire keeper though obviously dangerous, Africa introduces hers too young to a dire chase that will differ the home keeper from the one who will cook with their feet. An even more wounding endeavor suffered by those who took the hearth of the cooking flame for a thing one can elude for a quick plate. A thing that usually entangles one in too much grapevine broadcasts. Earning one two or three titles of the mocking birds.

So did little Thabo yoke the burden of fire keeper with intuition of his much asking. For he did expect a rise in rank even in his plate as he did rise in the office of a fire keeper. Replacing his brother meant he could contend for his kind of pieces of meat and the like. Yet he had to be taught by his mother a thing or two.

"Mama, does it mean now I will eat the chicken head because now I kindle the fire."

"No!"

A straight no, meant he had to enquire the more to take mete of the lack in parity with Kaelo's efforts. For his older brother for keeping the same office did get the chicken head with his drumstick.

"But Kaelo got the head with the drum stick and he said it was because he kindled the fire when you cooked the meat."

"It means he did not know."

She was quick to engage him for she knew of his much inquisition he was due and about to learn a thing.

"But he is big and he knows more things than me. So does it mean he does not know all things."

He did ask occupied the more by his failure to keep up his said job. He had the heart but experience did bring dress him with much ado for nothing. For now and then he had to be helped redo the same little task; again.

"Even I my child do not know all things."

"Mama, then who knows all things."

"Did you forget that you did ask the same question yesterday. What did I tell you about asking questions?"

"I don't know. Does it mean I am bad?"

"No my son, it means you are learning."

She knew he had to be consoled. It would do help him carry on the said discussion without loosing direction.

"The reason your brother goes to school it is because there are things he yet has to know."

"Things like what mama?"

"Things written in big books. Books that you shall read when you go to school next week. And things like your place in life."

Thabo like any six year old had a keen brain to make every last answer the source of his next question. A thing that means whatever word you say is a snare.

"What is his place in life?"

"He is the stronger brother. So, he needs more food to eat so he may do tough works with ease."

"So, it means whoever works the hardest had to eat the most."

"Of course Thabo. Now it means you know a lot more things than you have to know."

"What does that mean mama."

"It means you know your place in life. When you know your place in life you let the elder pass then you follow. And when you know your place in life you take the little piece so the elder may get the bigger piece to do a lot of work."

"Now I know my place in life."

"Yes my son, though in this world a few other know. So, they will confuse your doing good for stupidity."

"I will just do the good mama."

"Yes son, there is much peace in knowing one's place in life."

In the little metaphors and the small things in life. So, did Thabo yearn the more to know so he may proof self sure. A thing that means from hither forth he would o serve a pattern. A latter to right that wrong if he did see it happen. So, he did carry on with laborious ideal though he was still to naïve and ended doing much damage to the progress of the fire than kindle it.

It took patience. And even the more endurance to let him cover self in char just to earn the stern office of a fire keeper. Though with his skills, he rather would have played observer for a few more years. At least two more to be precise. But life offers none a chance to wait. So, whenever she was near and close enough to be of aid in any case of need, he had to be engaged in these things to foreknow incase favor escapes his hold. That for any that would burden him with his care he would be of use. Though small and spasmodically yeaning, any good hearted being would appreciate his trying. For the bull is among the calves so any African knows. It only takes positioning and waiting until the said time.

It meant he had also have to learn to pace and time self as he goes out to play. To play hard for the given time and to be home for this humongous chore so he may have a feel of playing a role. To be in his place in life. So that when opportunity calls, he may be made ready to endure the call. It has to begin somewhere and for him it had to be the hearth. Though in a man's hand. He would begin somewhere where he would just hold on to avoid the part from moving. Just to boggle the flattery of casting his mind about. But he was rise in a lady's world. And his man hand had to be stayed off mommy's immaculate ways, until he could command the narrations of a knife or punch dough to bake a thing.

He was in his place.

The Very First Week

The very first week did prove to have a rather chaotic surprise in store. Not just one but a few more. Though some are memorable two were worthy to mention for little Thabo.

Though a brand new world. One had to quickly learn how to navigate it for the due course. It had to be just seven years but some were obviously by the look of thing headed for twenty or so more years in the little circuitous march that was supposed to just take seven straight years. Some owed to the years absconded even before attempting the first like Goaba, and some to the damaging attempt of trying to fathom standard four. A thing that could make one complete a circuitous march of all the Kanye primary schools ending with a call to one or another duty. Or rarely due to sharing standard four with their own child.

A course for jesting; though acceptable by the standard.

Though ever so hard to believe. Among the terrible giants now and then you would find a gentle giant. Like Papolo and even Tipa. And among the giants you will even find a real playful giant like Nghogho or Kedibonye and Potekane. But a thing with giants is on a good sunny day they are like the most of the meekest but do cross them. For their statue paralleling the same of the primary school teachers means something . It means they pack the same power less the authority and when they are pressed they could burst.

So often did one Ratsie affectionately known as S'tlhakwane did soon find himself in the parloining of an angry big guy or to serve justice he had to scale one riotous guy often with a ridiculously huge stick. It was not different with Super the very first week of the year of ninenteen eighty seven. Super and S'tlhakwana's tussle began in the standard six class and it did start an uproar. The teacher being S'tlhakwana had to abandon the stick for he for a moment seemed porous with it. It untangled him. But Super Ramangwele was forthcoming. Sibro or Mojeje as Somhlolo was affectionately known by the many names did break a cheer. They cheered like ones watching a football match and S'tlhakwana knew he had to do better. But in the end did Super turn around and did the unlikely. He did run out of school yard and it was not until after a few solid weeks that he did return.

He did return to a heroes welcome.

Though of course he had to man up for a few strokes of the same S'tlhakwana to call the case settled. The noise of the battle in passages and corridors did call for another thing only the standard one could escape by the default of not desiring them to be caught in a stampede. That one cursed morning did all the teachers suddenly turn on all the school as they were in the midst of assembly and none escaped. Owed to Somhlolo's cheers or otherwise for guys line Mendi would not quite down without a beating. So the noise was surprised and there were no longer any big group discussions during break.

Another entanglement of a giant and Potekane had to be instantly suspended. Instead of spending his days in a quitting down he did return that very same week to settle another score. For it proved he was owed by one of the smaller standard six pupils. He usually being a gentle giant was also and enterprising behemoth of note. Making his often trips to Lobatse bargains as Thabo later got know. Owing to his too much loading Potekane never cleared standard four. But in the latter years did Thabo even had the audacity to remind him of his old scuffle or two. And one of the most profound one was from that first week of eighty-seven suspension.

Soon as it was announced during the morning assembly that he was suspended, the sooner he did show up at the school gate. As early as break time it proved Potekane was outside the school gate dancing to a double speaker double cassette radio. It was not the jiving that was trouble: but rather what he was spinning and juggling.

A form of a jack knife commonly known as three star or okapi.

It called for a quick calculus to know who did trouble him and how. And it was soon found out that one Ntheneke owed him money for a loaned belt. So, little Thabo had for the first time have to attend one or two emergency assemblies that are usually due. Yet this one did spark even the more much gossiping and much murmuring that they would boycott the beating. Yet it was not about the bearing for even the standard ones had to be cautioned. It did surfeit the masses though a few guys like Mosenki and Fakane did already boycott it literally by spending the entire time at the toilets. Though it behooved the principal or headmistress as it was not offensive then to call her so. Come Along in such instances did prove self a stern leader, for she did stand like a mother did interrogate a whole school. Her quick pressing words yeaning a thing for one did scream Ntheneke as the cause.

It was Mendi as one could tell. And as often as at other times that he got the whole school in trouble. This one time he did loose it of an impending massacre. They hoisted Ntheneke up and was thus cast for with least of amicability but there he was tussle and untucked. A thing that sold him cheap for more scorn for he had made bumpers on his head. His kinky hair was like the rays of a field. Well planted across the slope. He had some ironing to do though already fully dressed and in school. To all's disdain he had already quickly sold the belt to one often absentee called Thomena. There had to be a way. Potekane had to be called. Though twenty pula was a hefty sum then did Come Along motherly grant a lien for Nthekene to be the one chargeable with the twenty pula pay.

He did obliged. For he was soon no where to be found

So, Marangrang as Potekane was also affectionately known did vacate the vicinity of the school with his two utterly unknown friends. It was beyond the male teachers Come Along as mother knew.

And so was buried the first week with an early release. For it was the first Friday of the year. And many were obviously headed for the lands or farms to do engage it much damaging searing around the fire. Spewing chewed clusters of sweet reed or to the self branding exercise of making parched corn. A thing that often did mean they came to school with the skins of their shins peeling off or much blood held as dead bubbles in their shins giving that fashionable attribute of the moment being dipala. Some thing by no means have an English name. A thing that though seemingly dangerous oft has no abiding hazards to the legs nor do amount to any form of trouble. For the more blood did clot on the shin the more did the skin peel away to give way for a new growth.

This often shift between the two places did often leave the class lacking until the feastings and the farm produce is depleted. And but for a moment until the planting season that came in late August or early September there was another disturbance. But with the focus of the field for a moment lost. The sure promise of penene on Wednesdays and Fridays did for the most part of the year see a busy traffic to school to furnish one with it's detectability though it never came out of the kitchen in one predictable form. Whether turned in to porous porridge or holding as lentils it did satiate one as all.

So was sealed the first and they did quickly vacate the school to do go cast self in to the scant produce of the field for it hardly did ever rain those few long and horrid years.

The Offering

There was a strange thing happening during the first term.

The kids were to bring a piece of wood even though there was a delay. A delay not caused by the lack in supply: but a delay caused by demand. Sorghum being not just the staple food but also being the prime cause of inebriation. The government could not content to their competition for the skyrocketing price and was seen as the alternative option due to demand.

The supplier could hold.

Hold until the government do barge a little. A drought year has its own recourses. So, there was no food in the store as was no food in the kitchen. The little they had was used to lure in the standard seven pupils in hope they would endure the extra hours and even for some to keep at it until exam time.

It meant the newbies had to do an uncommon thing. Bring their own food from the onset. A thing more acceptable to the unlearned for the mature masses would rather labor through the day and eat later at home. But the fragile young had of necessity have to bring their own from the very first day. A somber start to the usually delightful pot washers. It did mean a demise to their usual enterprising that often do live them with stubborn stains on their school uniform. It meant Kaelo had to do the little more cooking to do accommodate Thabo's first dish. Meaning the cooking would be to much of their unnecessary occupying do have extra things to be cautious of.

Yet with or without the food the school was set to start as usual and it did go on.

Due to Miss Marumo's astounding and remarkably knowing edge. In his little mind Thabo could discern a thing. As the hard worker of his class, she did deserve a thing. To eat the bigger portion so she may be able to do best at her job; educating.

It took guts but Thabo being an astoundingly good hearted lad. He new he had to do something. Contrary to popular believe to him she was starved, for her portion of skinned chicken spelt dire to him. There little Thabo opened his lunch box and trembling he headed for the teacher's desk. In much obeisance he inquired of her. He did speak his every word with a bending of his knees. A profound exhibition of awe soon found Africa over.

"Mistress, may you have my piece of meat please."

She thus had to look a little yonder her table. Over her Mahoumed's ordered humongous sunglasses, that though were a shade or two towards black, much emulating spectacles; were just for show rather than for aid. For she still had her perfect vision perfectly set. She was lost for words. There was an utter silence for a while.

He could tell he was breaking the norm. Yet he needed the more to set the bar high. To high where all things would be so well set the class would be so well taught. Of impulse he did break personal one or two rules. For it being the age of scabies and big circle uncandidly formed there on the other side of his temple. And another sneakily set on the left of his nape. He often had to break the gentlemen's rule and to his disgust do an inordinate thing. Openly scratch it, casting a few debris of its much raffling of dead skin and dandruff.

More like a chicken raffling her feather touch one of the two he always had an effect. He did apologize.

"Sorry mistress, I did scratch the temple of my head."

It was not because he could see the restraint it is binding too hard his unfathomable mission. But to the much etiquette he had to learn of his mother to be gentlemenly.

"I will go out to scratch next time. So I may apply ointment on the patch."

It was not just a startling ideal but his impeccable innocence and the bold statement that he had just deliberated with it. She looked beyond him, to the crochet skin upon his little fit and the bare elbows though he was supposed to be wearing a hand knit school jersey. His older brother leaving primary the former year opened a hole in Their mother's Postal Savings Account. He had to get the resized clothes of his brother to afford his mother the candid ideal to afford his older brother a partly set school uniform.

She shriveled with an impediment.

An impediment just made deliberate by the lad's supposed ideal that in all his lack and obvious state of frailty. He weighed her supposed to have his piece of meat to provide a harboring lack that he esteemed empowered to deal with. She had a baby chicken skinned drumstick there cast impulsively upon her salad. There was a dress that was causing all this mess. She had ordered a size three dress and she was sure going to be stunning in it that is if she was to keep her diet for the said three months.

"Will you mistress."

He did ask extending his right hand where upon his two generous dumplings he had a charred drumstick. That one could identify as belonging to a cock for it was a bit too large to be one of a pair of a female. He swallowed hard with his eyes narrowed. One could tell the damaging the patch of scabby on his head was doing to his intent the lofty price he was paying to the efficacy of being etiquette. He had to scratch self but she was like an airplane due to a storm earth anchored.

He could not suppress it any further though it complicated the more her ordeal. He did use his little left hand to raffle the patch again. She is was baptized further deeper in to disdain and the loathing of his condition. She for the first time could tell, she has to know her place in life to do fathom her ideals and still be his favored.

It was during an era.

An era that soda water and mayonnaise were supposed to get one a few sizes less, that is if you could keep at it using mayonnaise for a dressing for a month or two while drinking the soda water for a wash down. But here was a thing. A thing that needed instant mitigation and a secluded adjudication.

The offering.

The offering offered by her first day pupil in front of a wide eyed class. The Teacher Training College intern was also beyond words. For she did not know what to make of it, and in addition to the little souls, she too was confounded by the happenings to the audacity of an expert chewed spectator, it was like she had seen a specter; a spooky thing. So she did not hold her peace but rather of a flabbergast, could not do a thing; she was in loose terms boggled.

So, Thabo reiterated one hand scrubbing his much scared scalp, for the age of scabbies here in Africa was not yet spent. Especially here home in Kanye. For already though the first day, a number of the pupils had already missed the first class due to the plagues of the draught, one being "makidiane" and the other "sompana" or "motshweetshwee". The said being a firm of infection that gives one a sore throat and the poxes in their deviant manners.

"Mistress, would you have my piece of meat."

She indeed was boggled. Lost for words. For even between the fingers there and then she could deliberately count the packed pox scars for he was in parting terms with a recent episode. Though receded, one could still pick one or two hang skin spots to the upset of the scrubbing stone commonly known as "lengwaelo". For to come to school he had to part of the common first term African school night ritual. He had to succumb to the much scrubbing by his mother using orange sack and the more fierce 'lengwaelo' that usually results with the need of a second consecutive bath to sedate one of the damaging effects of the first. The second bath is serine that is compared to the first where one has to loose a good weight of dead skin by the forced intrusion of a scrubbing stone. A thing that do upset the heels, for the checkered lines now become hanging hard skin that do effortlessly for the preceding week will generously peel away. A thing that would quickly deal away with a new pair of socks within a week if one had the luxury of owning a new pair with their Christmas surprise; a whole school uniform.

Despite the piece being in part charred. It was a commonality among the masses though distant from those who could afford a paraffin stove. Or the more educated a primer stove. For with the blanket of night fully covering the open African sky, the three legged pot and a raging wood fire, there is no way of avoiding soot: there has to be some charring to say you cooked it in the night.

The horrid bite of winter meant one had to sort a place to keep the fire kindled in a warm place. But January being the strength of Summery weather, an open sky did add the much to the idols or tales exchange that buried the evening hour in a quick passing joy. Always leaving a demand for one more idiom or flock tale. Just one more always came with an astounding please. And the merit of the open air and the generosity of the vagabond evening breezes meant the fire wood would much have part in the coloring, taste and the charring of the culinary.

She swallowed hard and she did swallow real hard again. Yet a bedimming mist was harboring her the intended honor she much desired to look in to his small plastic dish well. She felt an impulse, an impulse to shout but had no strength left in her so in surrender rather than in inquisition she was lowering her self back in the back of her chair. A thing that called for putting her cladding of the ridiculous sunglasses aside.

"Why?"

She asked failing the much to hide the ideal she was spooked.

"Because you work a lot hard to teach us. You deserve my piece because it is bigger than yours."

So she searched the means of justice to in an amicable manner deny the lad to give his offering. But he sunk her deep even the more in to his snare. One could discern the weight of a small mirror in Thabo's right pocket. A thing he obviously kept in the even where his impulse did manage to escape his mannerism. To do apply ointment again and deal away with flakes of his two scabby patches in a gentlemen's way. And to aid him direct the pasting of the ointment. For calamine and menthol seemed the only two solutions one could make for the many skin plagues.

One loathed for the smell and one for the color. For whether you have applied one of the two. These two did speak loudly, in essence one could not go anywhere until they have duly wiped away their dosage of calamine. And one had to be in the open for a few minutes to deal also with the breathe clasping effects of menthol to mix with any not taking the medication. He did speak from the fresh stink of his menthol application. A thing that buried him in the more rewarding relief of its rather too minty chill.

"My mother said I should know my place in life. For a bigger person needs the bigger piece to do a lot of work. Take mine so you can teach us even some more."

She knew she was in for it.

He was in all sincerity sent by an adoration, a form of comely affection for her stern service. With her having the internet playing watch; she did do her best. To do indoctrinate her in the way of the educator and to give her tall tales her impeccability. Was it all raining down due to this moment of indecision or what?

He was set on a course and it did not seem he would be an easy push over. And she was not going to tussle his mother the very first day, he leaves her care. She could tell he was a keeper of heroines. She had to agree with her in an amicable and responsive manner. She had to barge, to barge and do something before the offer turned in to something horrid or causing a torrent of tears. He was way too young and he was way out of her league. She had to do something. And the intern was not helping for in the gist of things she had already managed to mar her face with a few escaped tears.

Her New Look cream and face lotion marring much her visage. She cared none the less that she was in the presence of her pupils. One could tell she would rather not be any where else. This was her interacting with her place of work. And it did excite her beyond reproach. He was doing it for her. And one would ask: Was she a whiner?

Or it indeed do call for that kind of rain?

She found herself grappling with reality. For even herself at that distance she could do define the charring. A thing that she knew was robbing her superior of the deliberated gift; for upon a little char the evening did not do them justice. For an inordinate few tiny further did stick out and a few fur. The thing with dealing with the feathers of a Setswana chicken. You have to have the experience to finish off well: that is by the spasmodic fur. She herself was lost deep in the gist of things. He had managed to in that little time also harrow an impending sorrow in her. A thing she knew cannot be done that easy to her. For she had in the past seven years of her teaching experience seen it all.

He came as the sole fan who did not fear but rather venerated the ladies heroes.

He did not just lift the bar. He that instance wrecked it. Thabo was a brand new chapter, instead of confidence he was oozing humility born of a candid innocent heart. He did not mean to challenge her, but rather he did submit beyond his call for her. For she did find herself trembling of the terrible awe brought upon her by his innocent soul. It was not a tremble of terror but of a crumble, a thing that she knew she was about to mar her make up making a mess of her first day in front of the class. He was thus picking her from her lofty distant height; and he brought her to the awe of being worthy to share his honorable dish.

"I know I can't have the bigger piece. I know my place in life."

She did not do it of her much inquisition but rather to a debility that sprang in an impulse did ask after him.

"Where is your place in life?"

"I know I must learn from you to be as good as you."

She could no longer hold. So she yielded and the pangs of the harrowing sorrow so let loose her stream of her own. She broke down and sobbed gently. As she asked.

"But what will you have for you have one piece."

He boldly edged on.

"Your little piece. It is enough for me. I only have to sit down and listen and learn."

She abhorred the scheme of things.

The competition with her fellow teachers. The bureaucracy of being an ideal. An ideal of being the best, though it damages one's true self just to sedate the keeping of the visage among the company. They were destroying each other; health and other wise and the much squeezing to fit in to an elusive circle of a purported pattern of being. She felt so, so, so tired of it all and she knew what to do. He was a wake up call. A boisterous knock of God to say, "Where is your seed of innocence?"

There young Thabo stood to the hurt of self and to the damage of much ideals. For in that one moment, though he had a piece of meat, she could not simply bring her self to taking it from him. For by her own self set standards it was rubbished. Not rubbished of his capability, but a debility he had no power to fathom. For who would let him cook?

Yet he who was raised of the rubbished ordeal did afford her to learn a thing. She could not hold. She had to come to his level to be blessed by him. For in him was a blessing beyond the reproach of men: he had a pure and good heart. A thing that you will through a stone two or three stone through away in a crowd due to the drought and you will not find a man ready to let loose his morsel. Yet he was willing in his lack, not to just give but his best portion for less.

He yet with nothing was composed to stand for what he believed in, a desire to humble self so that he may loose his big piece. So that she may satisfy her soul, not that it would give him back a thing. But so that the ideal of the way of life may be attained, and his harrowing gushed an infallible foundation of guilt raining much ought to her many impediments. She was supposed to be the perfection that molds many. A mold and here she did ask herself.

"Am I a fit mold for the fashioning of a good new generation?"

She found herself lack. Yet she did proceed to go and hug him and of his ill health and many other impediments he did bring to the table. She had to see through it all to do grasp at the light burning through his little heart. A ray of hope crying for a torch to elucidate, for he was not just a boy but a messenger of good news and remembrance.

In trying to learn from her the more: he did teach her the first principle of all; to remember her place in life. Who she is, and what she left her people and her little scanty home village to become. An educator of profound status. A fountain oozing the infallible myriad possibilities of education.

She did reduce her self and did grab his generous dish and did accept to be baptized. For she was lost and by him she is found. She did mar herself a little bit being a daughter of Africa she would not let her tears surpass her cheeks. It was not just taboo: but an also an ideal she had to uphold even for the aspiring young. And with the dish in hand loosed of his rather petite stature she did assume again her sit. What Thabo lost aware of is that she was in possession of his dish.

The Source

Miss Marumo had a thing burning inside of her. A desire to see the source of the vehemently rampant virtue. She did sincerely sort a plan. A plan in conniving, to go and see Thabo's mother. For she too had an offer, an offer due to Thabo though she needed his mother's consent.

Abandoning the teachers' vine. That after its much deliberation often to the surrender of the cravings do the standard six and seven teachers do in the conniving send. To the tuck shop to buy fat cakes and a few chicken feet to munch away the bones with chewy skins of the fat cakes. Women!

Though all in a good heart and with his full dish as an exhibit in hand. That one blessed afternoon and horridly hot day she did at a discerning distance follow young Thabo home. A distance unseen one would say, so he may unknowingly lead her to his distant home. It did inebriate her in her horrid past of succumbing the distance between her distant lands and her school footing behind avid walkers. It was a chore on its own, fueled only by her ignited lamp of passion she so dearly beheld. For in the long unpausing scourge of the drought and the terrible winters she had to almost in a running pace do follow them to school. Until Junior School introduced her to the intricate system of a boarding school. A heaven that formed her in to the stern educator she had just remembered.

So, in Thabo she saw a thing.

A firebrand riotous with sparkles of infatuation. Before his bubble burst, she had to do put his head deep in the clouds. He was an influencer, a sure precursor to tie the many vagabond scoundrels to. If she would play a Samson; tying a fire to his 'tail' she could weaponize him to cause to be ablaze the whole field. She had to give him a ground and a place of his own. A place in her class to do cause others to follow his ways.

She knew it was not until around standard three that a class can have one or two play the ever illusive role of a monitor. A thing left to naught for they are often as forgetful as they can be. He did the obvious. When he did loose self of the school uniform he did assume his five liter water container and did make it for the stand pipe. During the days of water affairs and mostly during the eighties a home stand pipe was an unheard of thing. All had to assume the road for a tedious eclectic journey often adding up to more than one rout a day.

The source.

Allowing Thabo to do systematically of her much conniving escape her hold. She brought out his dish and worked a way of approach. And there she was straightening her hair with a stretching stone. Though sheen straight was not that expensive she had to place her two sons before her and all missing the ideal of indulging self even a little. The precious little things of this life were rather not a thing she aspired for, but to meet the ideals of raising two thoroughbreds being her first son and second son. Armed with blue seal Vaseline and sunlight soap. She would with the aid of a dire hot stone stretch her mane to the supposition of the current standard of beauty. A thing that was as common as a charcoal loading iron. Rather, luxurious then.

Seeing his dish she did let his name escape her lips with a herald of urgency.

"Ma'am, what did Thabo do?"

She asked bending her knees in reckoning. She sure was not in a position to play his defense though by all means she was already pleading for his course.

"Thabo!"

She sounded the herald again, though her posture and all were given to Miss Marumo. The exhibit of Thabo's dish did make run unrestrained the many and multiple possibilities he might be a culprit worthy to so quickly and directly apprehend. She did ask the more her hands occupied by her yeaning enterprise for she was without minding the care of a mirror or an aid on herself pleating her head.

"He is out, I saw him go out as I came in."

"Ok! Madam, you may take the seat."

She did with an obviously panicking amicability did oblige as she did offer the younger teacher her seat. She did excuse herself from her place to give her the gallon can for oil of USAID did come in five liters or gallons which could both be repurposed in myriad ways. It was not just about her immaculate pleating of self. She would on her own with all carefulness iron her whole head with the stretch stone, until it shines and straightness almost makes mockery of the hair relaxer proponent. A thing she learned out of the curve balls life often throws at one.

She was still overwhelmed by the presence of Miss Marumo.

It was not every day that a teacher did come to her home, let alone on her son's first day at school. Yet beyond what oe could see, her good son did move a lofty heart to her humble abode.

"You may have his dish. He forgot it on my table."

"Did he five you trouble Madam?"

"No, rather he reminded me of who I am."

"Oh! That's good Madam."

"You can call me Silvia or Miss Marumo. I am Thabo's teacher."

"Thank you Madam."

She saw no need to introduce her self. She did not weigh herself worthy to mention before such an education authority so she did quite her self down.

"You did not tell me your name. I would like to be your friend. May be you can pleat my hair like yours some times."

"Madam I don't know English. What will people say?"

"It is not about people. It is about the friends I choose. I believe you could give me good advice."

"What do I know Madam Silvia?"

"A lot more. Like kindness. I will buy Thabo his whole school uniform and you can pleat my hair now and then for a pay."

"I would do it for free my friend, that is what friends are for."

"Then is it a crime for a friend to help friend. At the end friends do have needs you know."

"I understand."

So, they we whipped off the ground by a gelling borne of the burden of being Thabo's dish home. And before he could return. Miss Marumo knew she had to as cunningly appropriate as it was to do vacate the place before she startles Thabo in case he present self suddenly by a quick return. She thought he had done enough for the day, and though he would be making two or more routs, it would be good for him to find her gone.

"You can in his absence do slip it in to his bag. I believe he would remember in the morning to check and might be startled that he lost his dish on the first day."

"I will. Happily."

She was already content to do the conniving for her new found friend. She did present her an envelope. Though it did spark a lot of silently dying resistance. At least she was taking from a friend, and Thabo on his second day at school he would be well dressed. For the day was not yet mature. She could get to one or two places before the sun retires to show up another morning.

She for one had never experience the joy of a full classroom. Her hard earn calculus and burden some writing born of a primer three class. Three solid years of Gaegolelwe did give her the accounting to balance the books of her tiny business. So she did pair the journey to the slaughter place with the buying of Thabo's uniform. Though it never did happen to her, for the course of seeing it so for her children did make the moment ever so joyous. As a primer three graduate, she did of her own education did strive to be an examples. She has never thought of dependability as an ability but a measure she would not be limited by. A thing well deliberated by even by her older son's books.

Though Miss Marumo did not say it.

She had already that quickly could discern Thabo was Kaelo's young brother. And the much virtue had a fountain. A fountain she herself did bend down to drink openly from. There had been a thing separating Kaelo from his peers. The immaculate covers of his books and the impeccable knit work to hold the hard plastic in place. Though not yet told, she could without an aorta of hinder tell. She had carefully covered them with the inside flour paper that in color emulates the khaki purchasable covering roll. And of the packaging plastic had made immaculate work of Thabo's books though instead of masking tape, she had carefully used sawing thread to hold the hard flour paper and the rather durable disposable cement pallet cover in place. Though of the humblest of sorts. Without any weave or hinder she knew it was Kaelo's young brother.

Though he had done graduate primary.

Still the more Thabo was an astoundingly similar replacement. She did not just yearn, but desperately needed to see the exponent of all this immaculate work. For she commanded the direct of reuse without saying a word. Like a silent orator, she spoke her terms with a delicate oration; service. She served her kids with a verve inordinate despite her obvious importunity, of her lack she made heroes of her children.

She of her own accord had set a place for her self in life. Though effeminate, it has been set in her own terms. To be a force and a reckoning to the aspiring young woman, who said I missed the door way to a formal classroom, in her own way. Though they had met once and a number other times. It was under the hazing pretext that she was the lead she was the obvious follower. Here parity earned her the warmth of her soul and she was due to come back soon and many other times.

Today was just a beginning

The Last Day

The first day of a term when one has found their place are rushed and do pass so quickly one cannot tell. So did Thabo's first term. With his teacher being his mother's friend. It did accord him a responsibility beyond his obvious placing. A responsibility to prove worthy of the much ado that did bring home a teacher on his first day from school. And indeed it was worth it. For he was bound to make a thing of the virtue pouring in to his life.

There did come that unusually exciting and dreadful day.

The last day of the term.

It is the only day where one can settle their score with any the quick and fastest way. For there was a preordained natural arrangement. The first being the picking of litter and eclectically packing away the desks and chairs. It is one of the days with the scantiest of advents. For it is a day many past hatchet should be shown before they are finally buried.

One well grown Onkarabile affectionately known also as Mkhezana or Senkhanana by the daring was an aid at distributing the rations usually afforded all the students to sustain them during the school holidays. He was not just an avid divider but also a stern scout. In his oversized shorts and a feet shaming any of the male teachers' shoe sizes he did do much good to earn his much rewards. For on the last but one day he did disperse the rationing, a thing that at its end burdened him with Benjamin's portion. To the masses not induced in the Biblical interpretation of the saying: he carried home five times plus anyone's portion. And so did a few of his friends. He was a guy tauntingly short though full of age and a voice capable of controlling the whole school without moving an inch.

Of all the aged, he was the shortest but the most well built. For even his service of usually eclectically washing the pots as did the other few giants every afternoon after school did carry an astounding 'samatudu'. A dagger like instrument made of the door frame's L shaped lower part that is usually pulled out when the door frame is inserted in to a building. There was no way you can conquer a sorghum emptied pot without it. For it was the only way to part it with 'patipati' or the compressed burnt base that is often the tastiest of the sorghum meal for once loosed of the pot, it assumes the design and form of a biscuit. It took skill and patience to gather it and it often got a few of them enterprising in an exchange of blows. A thing that usually amicably settle self, lest they be lose of the sacred enterprise. For temptation did get one to do the unintentional now and then.

These were the times when it was fine to chase someone and pull their fat cake out of their mouth for a share or total nab. The five thebe fat cakes were a highly desirous snack during break time. But with birds of prey like Kedibonye prying. One would soon spare their five thebe until the day he is not on sight. For he being a swift giant, was advantaged to do the unthinkable of the smaller guys' fat cakes. Which were usually large enough for an average guy to cast in to the mouth as they use their feet and hands to make away from the cook's site. For they prepared and served along the school menu by the same cook. It was a duty to do navigate out with a mouthful, for guys like Kedibonye and

Onkarabile would just nab the fat cake before one can munch twice.

The worse scenario being his jaws had to be pressed loose to pull the fat cake out. A thing that did cause much disappointment that one could not outrun Kedibonye, it did not carry enough water to reach the school disciplinary lines. It was just water under the bridge for the said giant had not many other weakness other than that when not toying with the small guys he would be competing with Nghogho doing the head stand.

Though untold the much let us return to the last day.

This is the day Onkarabile would be going around picking all sorts of weaponry set aside to do much damage to the owing to settle aboding scores. Meaning it being a day none brought their books to school, the weaponry would have to be harbored in often open places selling the owners cheap. Despite the many times there were confiscations, it never really amounted to nothing in the big end. It usually amounted to a quick lashing and the case is settled. Then at around ten O'clock after a thorough three or four times of litter picking she thus summoned the whole school by Come Along. She did stand there on the stoop before the school library and did shout.

"Hip!,hip!,hip!"

And the whole school did shout.

"Hurray!"

And so they would gush out of the assembly point and out of the school gate at the highest speed their little and humongous feet could carry them. Attempting in the self same process of evading harm and ducking and dodging from the quickly lashing danger to randomly give two or three parting short slaps, or a kick or any other form of temporal hurt that did bring out the worst in an African child the not detrimentally harmful way. To excite self for the obvious danger they did put self in. It was deliberate it was for the excitement. For in this day none brought a book let alone a writing implement. Just to say good bye the right way. The African way.

Until next term.

Don't miss out!

Visit the website below and you can sign up to receive emails whenever Bobby David publishes a new book. There's no charge and no obligation.

https://books2read.com/r/B-A-DOCGB-PYMID

BOOKS 2 READ

Connecting independent readers to independent writers.

Also by Bobby David

John and the Keeper
Chamber of Candace
King Cyrus' Sword
Sealed Book of Daniel
Touch of Eve

Standalone
A Place In Life